This igloo book belongs to:

....

Contents

Published in 2012
by Igloo Books Ltd
Cottage Farm
Sywell
Northants
NN6 0BJ
www.igloo-books.com

F021 0312
10 9 8 7 6 5 4
ISBN: 978-0-85734-655-1

Printed and manufactured in China
Illustrated by Mike Garton
Stories by Melanie Joyce

Stories for 1 Year Olds

igloo

The Bell on the Bus

Ring-a-ding-ding, goes the bell on the bus.
"Put out your hand, it'll stop for us."

Suzy, Jonny, Derek and Dot, get on the bus at the green bus stop.

Ring-a-ding-ding, everyone holds on tight.
The little bus swings to the left, then the right.

The red bus stops for Milly and Pete.
They pay their fares and find a seat.

Up the steep hill, the little red bus rumbles.
Brrm-brrm-chug, the engine grumbles.

Chug-chug-brrm, it's nearly at the top.
Walter's waiting at the blue bus stop.

Ring-a-ding-ding, it's a bit of a squash.
But down in the town, everyone gets off.

The little red bus goes, *vroom, vroom, vroom.*
Ring-a-ding-ding, it'll be back again soon.

Bath Time for Bo

One lovely, sunny morning, Bo was curled up in her bed. Mummy came into her room. "Wake up, sleepy head," she said.

Mummy gave Bo a cuddle and said, “It’s time for your morning wash. We’ll make the water nice and warm, then we’ll *splish and splosh.*”

Mummy got a big, bath towel and Bo's special fairy mat. "Let's put some water in the bath," she said. Then Mummy turned the taps.

Swoosh, went the bath water into the bath.
It swirled and went, *drip-drop*.
Then, Mummy turned the bath taps off and the water stopped, *plip-plop*.

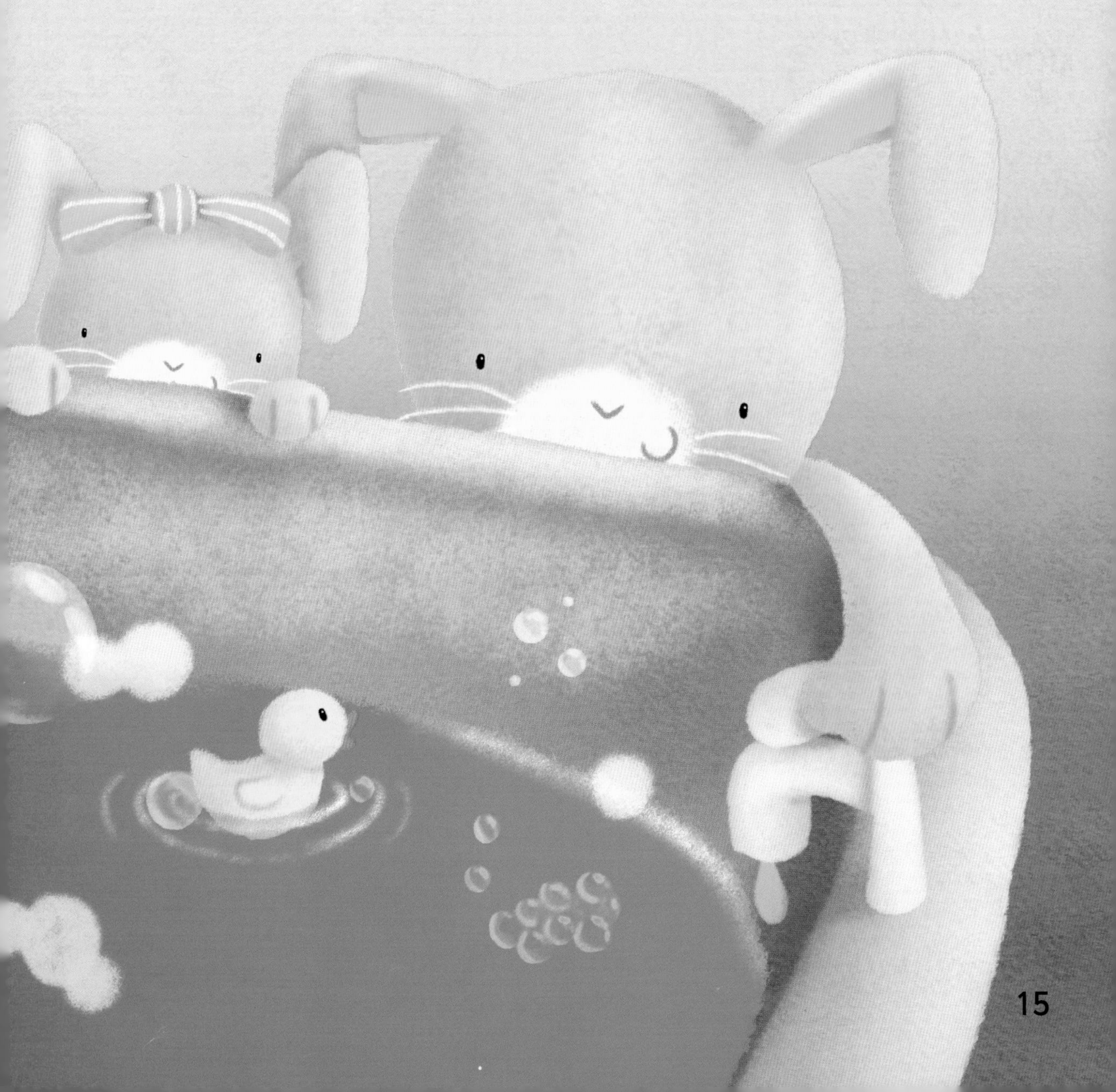

“There now, baby Bo,” said Mummy and she held Bo in the bath. She scooped some water on her back and it tickled and made Bo laugh.

Then, Mummy got the dolphin soap. She rubbed it on Bo's tummy. She pulled lots of silly faces. Bo thought Mummy was very funny.

Mummy got the big, bath towel and rubbed Bo's little toes. She dressed her in a babygro and wiped the bubbles off her nose.

Then, Mummy picked up Rubber Duck and patted him dry, too. “Look,” said Mummy to baby Bo, “he’s had bath time, just like you.”

Playtime Fun

Jenny is coming to Ben's house today.
Ding-dong, goes the doorbell. It's time to play.

Open up the toy box. Pull out all the toys.
There are beeps, squeaks and rattles.
What a lot of noise!

Here's a yellow digger, its engine goes, *brrm, brrm.*
Red racing car is very fast, it whizzes off – *vroom!*

Boing, boing, goes the little, blue ball, bouncing up and down. *Choo-choo,* goes the little train, chuffing round and round.

The red bus goes, *ding-ding*. The telephone goes *ring-ring-ring*. *Toot*, goes the car and *bang*, goes the drum. Making noise is lots of fun.

Tick, tock, goes the clock on the playroom wall. *Ding-dong*, goes the doorbell in the hall. Jenny's mummy has come to call.

It's time to put the toys away. "Never mind," says Mum. "You can play another day."

Jenny waves and says, “Goodbye, Ben. I’m glad you’re my best playtime friend.”

The Little, Blue Train

Everyone is patiently waiting on the platform of the station. The little, blue train comes, *choo, choo, choo.* It huffs and puffs and goes, *whoo-whoo-whoo.*

“All aboard!” cries the station master.
Soon, the train will be moving faster.

Clunk, go the doors and *click*, go the locks. The whistle blows and the train pulls off, rolling, rolling down the track. The little, blue train's wheels go, *clickety-clack, clickety-clack.*

Past the fields and the cows and the sheep. Up the hill that's very steep. Slowly, slowly, *chuff-chuff-chuff*. The little, blue train goes, *puff-puff-puff*.

Then it's down the other side, *whoo-whoo-whoo.* The little, blue train is rolling, *choo-choo-choo.* Through the tunnel, where it's all black, *clickety-clack, clickety-clack, clickety-clack.*

“Look,” says the driver, “we’re nearly there.”
The little, blue train puffs clouds into the air.
Then it slows, *click-clack*, on the railway track.

Slowly, slowly it comes to a stop.
"It's the end of the line," says the driver.
"Everybody off."

It's been a long day for the little, blue train. After a nice long sleep, it'll be back again. Goodnight, little, blue train.

Bedtime Frogs

It was nearly bedtime in the little frogs' house. "Hop upstairs," said Mother Frog, "and brush your teeth. Then, put on your pyjamas, it's time to go to sleep."

But, one little frog gave a big, dry croak.
He cried and said, "I've got a sore throat."

“I’ve got a sore throat, too,” croaked another. Soon, all the little frogs were croaking at their mother.

“Hush, now,” said Mother Frog. “Wait there, I’ll be back soon.” Then, she opened up a cupboard and got some medicine and a spoon.

Mother Frog's medicine was drippy, gloopy and runny. A spoonful each for all the frogs slid right down to their tummies.

Soon, all the little frogs were tucked up in their beds. Mother read them a story and kissed their little heads.

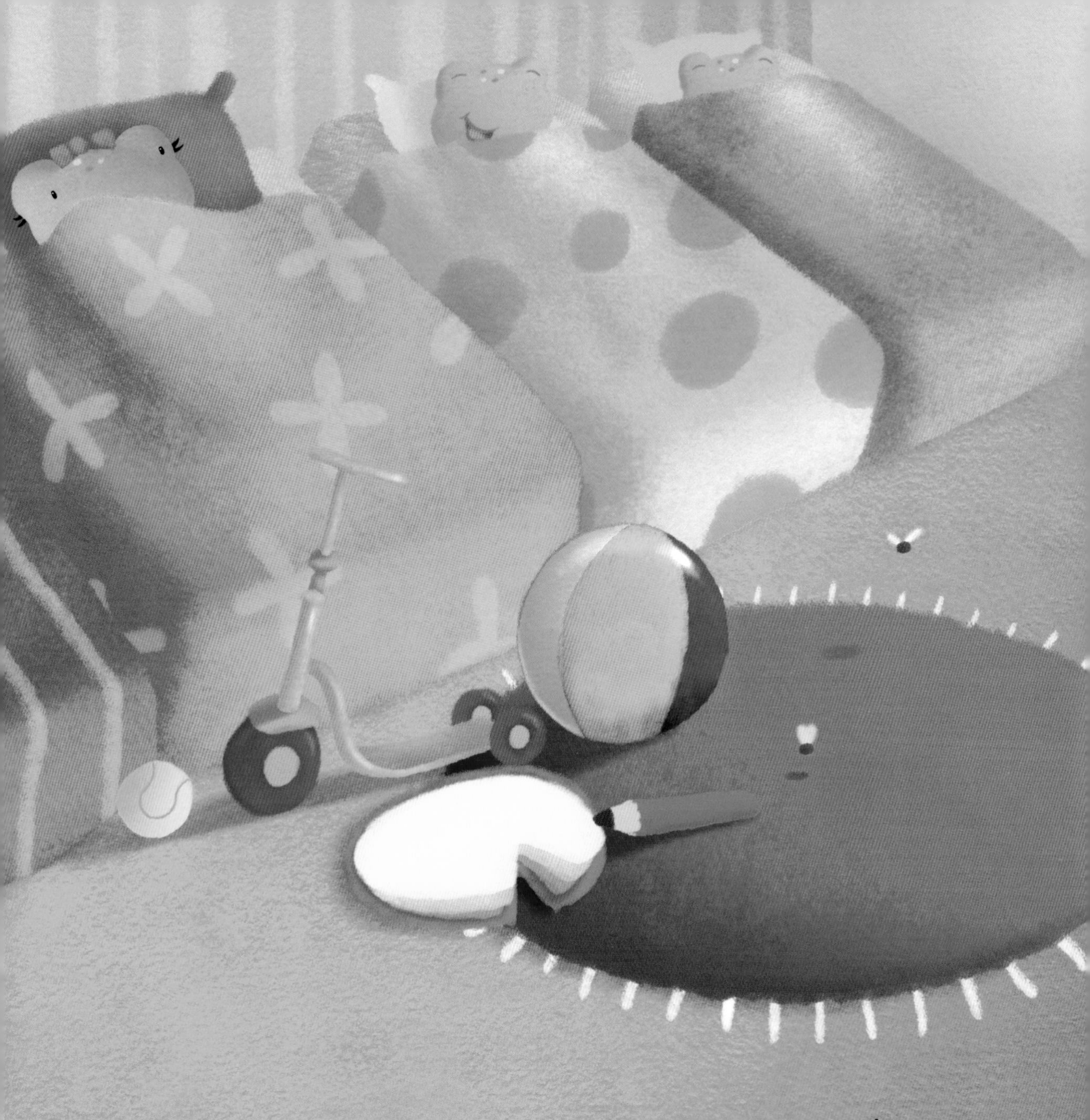

No one made a sound, as Mother turned out the light. All the frogs were very sleepy. "Goodnight, little frogs," said Mother, "goodnight."

Where's the Moon?

Lionel looked out of the window one night.
But there were no stars, or bright moonlight.

"Where are the stars?" he asked, "And where's the moon? Are they gone forever, will they come back soon?"

"They're busy putting the sun to bed.
But you can call to them," Mummy said.

"All you have to say is, *come out stars, come out moon, shine your light in my bedroom.*"

So, Lionel called to the moon and the stars.
And all that night he had sweet dreams,
sleeping under starlight and soft moonbeams.